Chocolatina

by Erik Kraft

illustrated by Denise Brunkus

Troll
BridgeWater Paperback

This edition published in 2003.

Text copyright © 1998 by Erik Kraft.
Illustrations copyright © 1998 by Denise Brunkus.

Published by BridgeWater Paperback, an imprint and trademark
of Troll Communications L.L.C.

First published in hardcover by BridgeWater Books.

First paperback edition published 1998.

Produced by Boingo Books, Inc.

Printed in the United States of America.

10 9 8 7

Library of Congress Cataloging-in-Publication Data

Kraft, Erik.
Chocolatina / by Erik Kraft: illustrated by Denise Brunkus.
p. cm.
Summary: Tina eats so much chocolate that she wakes up
one morning and finds that she has turned to chocolate.
ISBN 0-8167-4544-7 (lib. bdg.)   ISBN 0-8167-4736-9 (pbk.)
[1. Chocolate—Fiction.] I. Brunkus, Denise, ill. II. Title.
PZ7.K85843Ch 1998
[E]--dc21   97-34304

To Jack, with thanks
—E.K.

For Trinka and Toulouse—determined and true
—D.B.

Tina loved chocolate more than anything in the world.

She loved it more than birthdays, more than roller skating, and definitely more than dried fruit.

Everyone called her Chocolatina.

When Dad asked, "How would you like your eggs, Chocolatina?" Tina always said, "With a bowl of Choco-Crunchies, please."

When the lunch lady asked, "What kind of milk would you like today, Chocolatina?" Tina always picked chocolate milk.

And when Mom said, "Tonight we have
fruit salad for dessert," Tina covered hers
with chocolate.

Tina's health teacher, Mrs. Ferdman, hated chocolate and everything else that children liked. "You should eat only foods that are good for you," she told the class. On special occasions like birthdays or full moons, she gave them all dried prunes.

Mrs. Ferdman's favorite saying was: "You are what you eat." She would write it on the chalkboard and make the children repeat it every day at the end of class.

One day, during this part of health class, Tina bit the ear off a chocolate bunny. Then she stood up and said,

"I wish that were true!"

That night, a strange thing happened.

When Tina woke up, she felt all stiff.
She went downstairs and looked in
the mirror. Immediately she saw why.
"I've turned into chocolate!" she cried.

"Whatever you say, Chocolatina, dear," said her mother from behind her newspaper. "Now hurry up and eat your breakfast, or you'll miss the bus."

When Tina got on the school bus, everyone gasped!

"Do you mind if we don't sit together today, Chocolatina?" her best friend, Patty, asked. "My mom will ground me if I get chocolate on my new shirt."

After a lonely bus ride, Tina was glad to be in spelling class—her favorite subject. But her first word in the spelling bee was "cocoa," and she got so flustered, she spelled it wrong.

At lunchtime, Jimmy Delrooney tried to bite off one of Tina's elbows. "I just wanted dessert!" he told the principal.

Recess was horrible. Tina was too stiff to run or jump, so she had to just stand and watch everyone else have fun.

When it was time to go
back in, her feet had melted
to the hot pavement. The
other children had to carry
her back inside.

Worst of all, it was time
for health class.

Mrs. Ferdman made Tina stand at the front of the classroom.

"Didn't I tell you, class? What have I always said?"

"'You are what you eat,'" said the children.

"That's right! See me after class, Tina."

When everyone else had left, Mrs. Ferdman began to laugh. "I hoped this would happen. I hoped you wouldn't listen to me. I hoped you'd turn into a chocolate girl. Do you know why?"

"Why?" asked Tina, who was shaking so hard she thought she might crumble into a pile of chocolate chips.

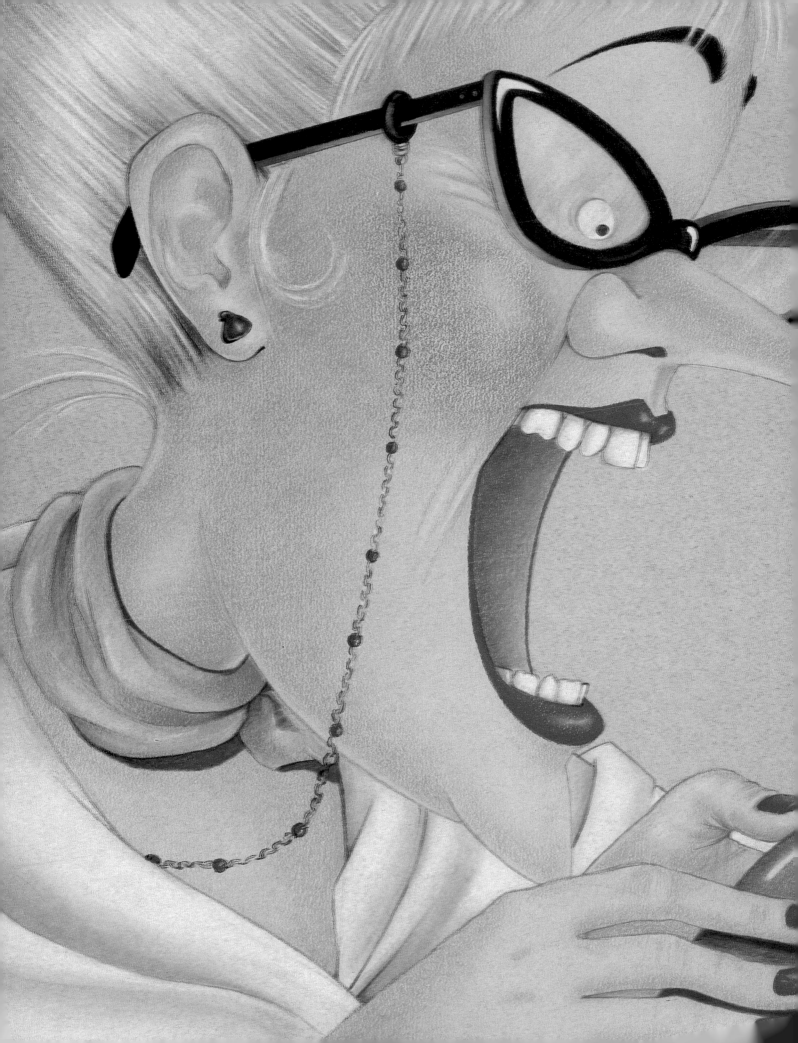

"Because I love chocolate better than anything!" shouted Mrs. Ferdman. She grabbed Tina, opened her mouth wide, and went straight for Tina's right ear.

Just then the principal walked in. "Mrs. Ferdman,
I was wondering . . . MRS. FERDMAN, WHAT ON
EARTH ARE YOU DOING?"

"I . . . I thought she was a prune," said Mrs. Ferdman.
The principal walked Mrs. Ferdman outside, and she
was never seen at the school again.

That night, safe at home in her bed, Tina cried a little chocolate syrup tear. "I wish I could be a normal girl again," she whispered.

And when she woke up, that was just what she was. "Hooray!" she cried. "I'll never eat chocolate again."

"Hurry up and eat your breakfast, dear, or you'll miss the bus," called Tina's mother.

On the table was a giant bowl of Tina's favorite super-chocolatey cereal.

"I'll never eat chocolate again," said Tina,
". . . starting tomorrow!"
And she ate it all up.